About Amitabh Sinha

Amitabh Sinha has been writing since his school days. During school and college days he was famous for doing write-ups for others who performed in debates. He also writes scripts and dialogues for stage performances. He has been writing Short stories, Poems and Novels in English and Hindi. He works for an MNC and ensures that he finds time to talk a lot to his son and his friends to get plots for his stories. His current work focuses more on child behaviour and skills. He tries to bring back the lost stories and ecosystem with his stories and presents it with today's life.

Adventures of Pupu

Adventures of Pupu

AMITABH SINHA

Kalamos Literary Services LLP

Kalamos Literary Services LLP
Email: info@kalamos.co.in | editorial@kalamos.co.in
Published in 2018
by
Kalamos Literary Services
ISBN- 978-93-87780-21-7

Cover Designed & Typeset in Kalamos Literary Services LLP

Print and bound in India.

1
God's Gift

"God is behind the clouds, and he keeps watching you, me and everyone," Pupu's mother told him once when she caught him stealing and eating sugar in the kitchen.

"So, does he live behind the clouds?" asked the curious boy.

"Yes, behind those thick clouds, he keeps watching from somewhere from behind the clouds," replied his mother. She further added, God is the provider, and we should not tell a lie to him. We can ask whatever we want from him; he provides us reasonably.

Pupu, a 6 years old boy, lived in a small town. All the houses of his colony were built very close, and all the roofs were accessible as they were joint. Pupu used to spend most of his leisure time on the roof. He liked watching the sky, clouds, and kites and eagles flying very high. He always thought those eagles were God's pet and so they flew near to the clouds. He always wanted to reach to them. And thought maybe he could make friends with one to know more about God.

Or ask for help to reach beyond the clouds and see God.

But he knew that the friendship with eagles was difficult because he had never seen an eagle come down to land. Also, the language would be another difficulty.

But he thought a kite could reach as high as a cloud. His neighbor, Som, a 10-year-old had always been a good friend. Som was a very good kite flyer. Pupu planned to learn to fly a kite from him.

Right after his school, Pupu went to the roof and as per plan Som was already there. The kite was already launched and was flying high. Pupu came excitedly and asked to hold the reel. Som gave him the reel and also gave some tips, "if you loosen up the line the kite will fly further but to give it the height, you have to roll the reel back."

"Look, if you have to control your kite, you will have to hold the line, this gives you the control over your kite against unexpected wind change," Som added further.

"I just want to know how I fly it higher to reach to the clouds," Pupu questioned in a loud voice to cut the heavy wind noise and make his question reach to Som's ears.

"Oh! That's too far, you need lots and lots of line," Som replied without looking at him as he was busy controlling his kite.

"How much?" Pupu wanted to know.

"Maybe as much as five reels. Do you know the distance?" Som replied and questioned him.

"Not exactly, but it looks like it is a distance too far than the nearest well's depth. I know the longest rope, my mother told me once, is required to fetch water you know," Pupu tried connecting somehow the farthest and the longest.

"Can you give me the line to hold once?" he asked Som.

Som handed over the line asking Pupu to be careful as there were other kites wanting to cut their kite.

Soon Pupu realized that one kite that was flying high was now suddenly flying free and going beyond all the kites. It was flying as high as the water tank tower. And now suddenly it passing the water tank tower.

"What is happening with that kite," Pupu was curious to know.

"Oh! That? I told you other kites could cut your line, that kite has been cut, and so it's flying free," Som answered.

Pupu then gave the line to Som and was silently watching the kite which was cut. He saw the kite flying far and far. He saw the size of the kite was reducing. He knew it is going far and very far from other kites. Soon the kite was not visible.

He went home and kept thinking about that kite. "Where did it go? How could he find it? Would he be able to find it? Who would have found it? Has the kite got stuck somewhere in the sky, between the clouds? Will it ever come back to earth?" After dinner, he was sleeping between his mother and father. He turned to his father and asked, "Papa, kites that cut out of their line, where do they go? Do they come back ever?"

"Yes, my son they do come back, they fall down to land," his father replied turning to the other side to avoid any further silly questions like this and sleep.

Next day he planned to take more tips on learning to fly a kite.

After school, Som and Pupu met on the roof. The wind was good to launch the kite.

Pupu lifted it for Som and soon kite was in the air. And after some ups and downs in the wind Som was able to control it and make it stable and fly high.

Pupu shouted, "Fly it higher, higher, and go more, more, loosen the line."

Soon the kite was flying higher than all others.

Som gave the line to Pupu to hold.

"Just try pulling it towards you and see how the kite moves," Som continued with his lesson.

Meanwhile, Pupu broke the line string when Som got busy with something and was not looking at him.

And the kite was free, flying towards the other end of the sky beyond the water tank tower.

"Oh! What did you do?" yelled Som.

"Nothing, it just broke," Pupu avoided eye contact and replied innocently.

"We lost the whole line of string, how will we fly kites now?" Som showed disappointment.

"I am really sorry, I don't know how it happened, but I promise to buy you a new one," Pupu showed the same ignorance and innocence again.

Both went home. While going back, Pupu was looking at the fading view of the kite. He was happy within as he believed that the kite would reach to the God and come back.

For the next few days, every morning he went up on the roof to search the kite, but it was not there. He kept thinking many things.

Has it reached to the God yet? Did it come back? If it had come back, did someone take it? Should he ask someone about the kite? Was that bigger cloud correct address where the kite was heading?

After many such questions, he concluded that God might be unaware of who had sent him the kite. Hence, he was unable to return it.

He went to his mother and asked some money to buy a reel, line string, and kite. He went to the shop near the Park market where he looked at many colored, beautiful and designed kites. But he bought a white colored kite and other things and also one red ink marker pen with a thick point.

He went to his room and closed the doors. His mother was around and saw him coming in with a kite and all the other stuff and closing the doors. She silently followed him and sneaked from the window. Pupu was writing something on the kite.

He then went on the roof, and after some time he came down happily.

His mother saw him coming down, without his kite, she asked, "where is your kite, have you left it on the roof, someone will take it?"

Pupu never considered that he was being monitored, he fumbled, "ummmh! uahhm! Yeahh! It's there, there with Som." He lied very unconvincingly.

He was lost rest of the day, but he was happy within. He has made no mistake in writing a note to God on the kite. He has mentioned his name, his colony name, his mark of his roof 'near the tallest papaya tree' so that God would identify his house while sending the thing that he has wished to have from him, and most importantly he had flown the kite high and cut the line to reach to the clouds. He was now waiting to get the wish fulfilled.

Next morning when he got up rubbing his eyes, he found 'the electro quiz' beside his pillow, that was the thing that he had wished for and communicated to the God. He saw around to look for God, but no one was around. He stood up with the electro quiz in his hand and started jumping and yelling on the bed – "mom, papa, come here soon, look, look at this, the God has sent me a gift." His parents appeared in the room. He said, "Look Papa, I got electro quiz, I asked God to send it, I wrote him a note on my kite and sent it behind the clouds, he lives there. You know mom, you are right, he lives behind the clouds."

"Yeppiiee, I am very happy. I am going to send God a thank you note today," he ran out to the courtyard and looked up towards the cloud. His parents also came there at looking each other and passing smile and feeling happy for their son.

Pupu again bought a white kite and wrote a thank you note to God and flew the kite high towards the cloud and cut it to reach the clouds. He watched the fading view of the kite to ensure that it has reached to the clouds.

He went out with friends, talked all around to tell the whole story to them and show his electro quiz.

He was acting like a leader of the group; he was narrating the whole story to every one of his friends. He was quoting God as his new friend. He said he could ask anything from him. He asked electro quiz from God, and he has been sent one. He was flashing his electro quiz to all his friends. But he did not tell anyone how he communicated with God. All the boys were behind him; they were interested in knowing how Pupu got the electro quiz and also seeing how electro quiz can be played.

He was busy playing with the electro quiz and telling how he got it to all his friends for a month; he never turned to fly kites.

One evening, he saw one of his friends, Golu, has got a new bicycle, and it was shining red in color. The beautiful orange color reflector was tied to the spokes of the wheel. Silver color bells and handle added to the beauty of the cycle. He touched the cycle, and it was such a good feeling that Pupu wanted the bicycle for himself. He asked Golu to give him once to ride. But Golu denied. Pupu felt very bad and pushed him from the bicycle. Golu got hurt badly on his head; he was bleeding and crying. Pupu ran home seeing this. Other boys ran to Golu's home to inform his parents. Golu was taken to a hospital, and after first aid he was relieved. Pupu's mom got the complaint from Golu's parents. Pupu was hiding in his room out of fear. His mom called him out to inquire. Pupu was acting smart to hide and tell all lies to prove himself innocent. But his mother was aware that he had committed a mistake.

Pupu did not go out of his house for a few days. He stayed on the roof with Som. After a few days, the situation was normal, and his parents were calm too. He asked his mother to buy him a kite. But she showed no interest in listening to him. After much of persuasion from Pupu, she gave him money.

Pupu again went inside his room with the new kite and closed the door. Her mother again sneaked from the window and found him writing a note to God.

Pupu followed the same way and came down happily without the kite.

He woke up the next morning but found nothing in the room. He went out, searched below the staircase, in the garden, in the storeroom but could not find the thing he had wished to get from God. He was a little disappointed. But thought, let's wait for a day or two.

But he got disappointment the following days too.

In the evening, he was very sad and sobbing in his room when his mother came in and asked what the matter was.

Sobbing he described that he wanted the same bicycle and wrote a note to God on his kite. The kite did reach the clouds. But his wish was not fulfilled.

"Are you sure God still lives there," he asked to re-confirm.

"Yes, he lives there only and as I said he watches everyone from behind, and all our conducts- be it good or bad," replied his mother.

"If he lives there then why is he not giving me the bicycle I am longing for?" Pupu questioned.

"I told you, God is the provider, and we should not tell a lie or do misconduct. We can ask whatever we want from him; he provides us reasonably," his mother explained.

She further added, "Check within you, have you done any misconduct, told a lie?"

Upon this Pupu started crying loudly and embraced his mother tightly and started confessing – "I have pushed Golu, and he got hurt… *sob... sob…*, I lied to you that I did not do anything to Golu, I am sorry… *sob… sob…* I have done a misconduct. I am very sorry, but I want that bicycle. Please God, give me the bicycle, please God, *sob… sob…*"

"You have to say sorry to your friend Golu and not to God. Once you say sorry from your heart, God will see it from the clouds, and your wishes will be granted," his mother said in a strict but a consoling voice.

The next evening, Pupu went out and apologized to Golu and his parents. He promised to be a good friend. He was happy and feeling light after this. That evening both played together and went home before the dusk.

When he reached home, he hugged his mother and thanked for helping him to make friendship with Golu again.

His mother fed him his dinner and took to the bed. His father was already there. He just turned to his father's side and asked, "Papa, will God forgive me for my misconduct and telling a lie?"

"Yes, of course, if you promise to be honest and just always," his father replied.

"And... and will he give me a bicycle now?" he asked again.

His father looked into his mother's eyes, and both smiled. They hugged their son, patted on his back asking to sleep.

Next morning was Sunday, they all went to the market to buy a bicycle for Pupu.

Activity: 1

Can you help Pupu? You know Pupu compared the distance to the clouds with the depth of the well. Can you help Pupu letting him know how can he measure distance?

2
Ghost of Jujube

Pupu was trying to reach to the branch of the jujube tree near the pond in the Phatic babu *bagaan* (garden) near the Durga Mandir road.

The *bagaan* (garden) now was just the remains of something that was once famous and beautiful. It now was just the ruins of a garden. The hedges had grown like small trees, and the ornamental plants had become so big that after dark people were afraid to go there as they mistook them to be a ghost. The *bagaan* now only had those plants which did not require care but can still grow and flower. *Kaner* (Oleander), Night blooming jasmine, *Champa* (Plumeria), *Naagfani* (a type of cacti), *Naag Kesar* (Mesua ferrea) were among flowers once maintained beautifully, but now they had grown on their own, and now were spreading like the bush in the jungle. *Dhatoora* (Stramonium), *Sadabahar* (Vinca), were some of the spontaneous plants that were grown anywhere in the garden.

Jujube, tamarind, guava were some trees that had grown very big, and no one ever dared to climb up. These trees were always very fruitful. They were always laden with fruits in season. The tamarind trees had grown as big as any monster. The guava trees were many, and of both the varieties- white and pink inner crust. When the fruits were ripe, the aroma of guavas spread till the road. The jujube trees were all spread on the edge of the pond. The pond was once very deep. But now the water level has gone down, and a big ditch like shape needed to be crossed before reaching to the water. The slope of the ditch was very steep, and most of the jujube trees have grown on the wall of the slope. This makes them difficult to reach for any human. These trees got loaded with lots and lots of jujube as they were challenging to be plucked.

People also talked about seeing ghosts at night in the *bagaan*. People avoided taking the nearby Durga Mandir road to their home in night although that was a shortcut. People often talk of gardeners who previously worked in the bagaan and were dead now, their ghosts still roam in the garden to guard the fruits and flowers. They were known to be staying on the big tamarind tree and on one of the Jujube trees which had the tastiest and big jujubes. This tree had grown such absurdly that reaching nearby was very difficult. Rain has made a big drench on one side of the tree, and a big land mass of the slope was washed away due to heavy rain draining on the other side of the tree. This had made the placement of the tree very difficult to be explored. Due to the drench, the land was very fertile, and so the tree was most densely laden with jujubes on it.

Leaving this jujube tree, people picked jujubes from other trees. Some urchin pelted stones and tried collecting when they hit well to make those jujubes fall on the ground. But those who pelted the stones couldn't always claim the fruit. It required to be managed properly between pelting stones from the base or top of the slop and running up or down for collecting jujube. In addition to that, there was no guarantee that the jujube would fall to the ground or in the mud nearby.

Managing between pelting stones and collecting jujubes often led to quarrel among urchins. And the winner was always the one who led the group in case there is only one group pelting that day, or belonged to a powerful group of urchins when there are many groups gathered on a day. Power was always related to being notorious or the number of lads in the group you belonged to. This was usual, but then mostly the one who picked the jujube was also considered winner, but not always, because the other group or individual may also have jumped at the same time to catch hold of the jujube, and pushing and snatching always was the deciding factor then.

Pupu was also part of one of such groups. But recently when he collected lot many jujubes in the event of stone pelting by two groups, one his group and the other was rival. While dividing the jujubes, his group leader took most of the jujubes and gave very little to him. While going back, Pupu got trapped by the rival group, and they tried snatching his jujubes. Both groups had a big fight, and his group managed to get back a few of his jujubes, but they did not give it to him and went along eating themselves. He tried telling everyone to give him his jujubes, but all laughed along and ate all. He was the shortest of all the group members and so was always deprived of his share of anything.

Pupu always had compunction within that he was not given the righteous share of anything in the group and considered of no importance although he had been participating in all the games, stint - be it good or bad, equally. He always thought that because he was short and lean, he was weak in comparison to other boys of his age, and it was always better to be part of the group. But now he decided to do all alone from now. This being the season of jujubes and he or any other urchins' groups had no other work but to try pick jujubes these days. He thought he would go alone to the expedition of collecting jujubes. He targeted the ghostly jujube tree which was not at all been targeted by anyone because of fear of ghost and the difficulty to reach to that tree.

Pupu knew that ghosts appear in nights only, so he planned to target in the morning hours. Pupu choose this tree to explore and prove his ability and superiority over others. He went early in the morning when no one was around so that nobody knows in case he fails and be safe from humiliation. He first tried to reach from the upside of the slop, when he was going down, he found that it was not easy to maintain the balance and speed with which he fell down. He was unable to control and stand anywhere near the tree. After multiple attempts, he decided to climb up from the bottom of the slop. He reached to the bottom of the slop from other safe side and walked all round to the side of that tree. Now he tried climbing up; it was like mountaineering. He had to manage the balance to maintain the gravity to stay still and walking up. After reaching half of the way, he realized that he was going towards the drench where it was not easy to cross and reach to the tree. From the other side of the tree, it was too high for him to get up to the tree from the depth of the ditch created by the flow of rain. He now knew that he would require someone's help, or some articles like rope, big stones to make way till the tree. He decided to try again the next day.

When he reached home, he was tired and hungry. He asked mom to give him breakfast. When his mother saw him covered in dirt, she asked him to take a bath first. He went to the well and fetched water for himself and took a bath. While taking a bath, he decided to take the rope used to fetch water from well the next day to climb up till the jujube tree.

The next morning, he reached the site with the rope. He took a look from the point he was trying to reach to the tree and ruminated how best to use the rope. The rope was not long enough to be used from the bottom of the tree. He planned to climb some distance and then use the rope. He saw some people coming and hushing him by saying, "don't you know this tree is a ghost's house? Stay away from this tree." But he remained there until those people were gone. He then started again.

He used several tricks and attempted to tie the rope to a nearby bush and climb step by step near to the jujube tree. It was afternoon when he started sweating in the month of February. He took off his sweater and tied to his waist. After taking rest for a few moments at the halfway, he started again. Pulling himself up, untying the rope and tying again to the next highest bush and then again pulling himself up. Stepping up with utmost care on each step without making any mistake or he would fall to the bottom of the pond with no one to rescue. At some steps, he slipped but very swiftly managed to save himself from falling.

He was growing strong in his head. The strength within him was increasing as the distance between him and the jujube tree decreased. He knew that this part of the land was unclaimed, untouched and he was going to be successful and gain honor. Now it was not just a question of eating the tastiest jujubes but was a question of winning and showing his ability by reaching the jujube tree. He was about to reach to the trunk of the jujube tree and was so thrilled in the action that he jumped directly from a far distance to catch hold the trunk of the tree, but his head knocked somewhere and started losing consciousness. He watched himself fall, and as everything turned dark, he saw a white-clad man appear tearing bright light beyond the jujube tree. He was very tall and had very long hands. He was smiling and extending his hand towards him. Pupu was afraid a bit thinking this to be the ghost of the jujube tree but was not ready to step back for the reason he did not want to lose the ground that he had just won. He wanted to have the fruit at any cost now. While the hands were reaching him to hold, he made his body stiff and heavy so that he couldn't be lifted easily. He was still falling, but with this stiff body and arms, he held himself at some place.

All in his unconsciousness he could hear the voice of the man – "You have won my boy. You have won over the ghost named 'fear.' You have won over the ghost named 'dreadfulness.' My dear boy, you know! People who thought and spoke of ghosts on the tree are not worthy of yummiest of the fruits. People who dare to break the barrier and stretch to go to any extent to get their dream fulfilled are the most deserving to get the sweetest fruits on the earth. Come on!

Come on, get up my boy, get up and enjoy the yummiest jujubes of life now. You have won over your shortcomings."

Pupu slowly opened his eyes and found himself on the branch of the jujube tree he was tightly holding and the branch was densely laden with jujubes. There was no one around. He was happy and wished everyone to see him there. He won the fear within by killing the ghost of jujube.

Activity: 2

Can you draw and color the *Sadabahar* (Vinca) flower?

3
Tipsy – a Hero

Wandering aimlessly he was tired, thirsty and hungry too. He had been searching the place where he could get some food and shelter.

When he headed towards a lane in a town hall colony, he got surrounded by stray dogs of the place. They chased him growling and grumbling. Some tried to bite him, he in turn bit some. He tore some and was torn too. He then tried sleeping under a tree in the gold ground, but urchins flung stones at him. It was annoying for him; he had always been loved and cared for by all. He had no clue why the whole world had become so weird towards him. Since his childhood, he had never experienced hatred or been misbehaved by anyone.

He then left for the Park market by the wide lane and strayed into the crazy lanes saving himself from rushing cars and bikes. He managed somehow to save himself falling into a dirty sewer while escaping from getting under a rushing bike. But he could not save himself from getting some dirty stains on his snow-white fluffy hair. He was a Japanese Spitz breed of dog, with white fur as snow and black eyes and nose which gave him all the beauty to be fondled by anyone. But wandering in the city for the whole day, he had lost his white color, and road dust had covered his whole body, with patches of dirt stains here and there.

It was dusk now after a whole day of floundering. Moving further he then landed in a filthy lane. The lane had no lamp posts. There was some dim light from the kerosene lamps that hung inside the shops. This part of the town was unknown to the average citizen, but he was drawn there by the smell of meat sizzling in tandoors. People drinking country liquor and merrily assembled there. The clatter of mincing meat on iron frying pans kept the environment lively. He stopped at the first shop. Somebody threw him a delicious bit of kebab-- and more came. The feast went on all night. People were generous there. There were dozens of other dogs, but there was no trouble since the territory did not belong to any gang in particular, and the stuff to eat was in abundance, and everything was delicious. He found everything so satisfactory that he decided to spend the rest of his life here- far away from his master's servants. In about a week he had become the favorite of the place.

The charm, however, did last for long. He had lost his appetite. He never touched the kebabs thrown at him. He really preferred to go without food. He hungered now for his master's company. But he knew his master has gone out for long. He does not like to stay with the servants. He decided to enter any house in the locality with similar looks and luxury.

One morning Shivani was sitting in the garden and sipping a cup of tea when she felt a cold touch on her feet. She looked under the table and shrieked. "Rascal, where have you come from?" He curved his hind in half, tucked in his tail, and stood before her with bowed head. Shivani shouted to call the gatekeeper. She demanded, how the hell did this dog enter the compound. The gatekeeper was unaware and stood in mute. The gatekeeper took the dog with him. As soon as the gatekeeper was about to throw him out, Pupu emerged from somewhere and asked to leave the dog alone. The gatekeeper said that Pupu's mom had asked to throw the dog out. Pupu rushed inside the gate and reached the place where his mother was sitting. He requested to keep the dog saying, "Look at him mom, he seems to be lost and needs a friend." Shivani accepted on the condition, "we will not allow him inside the house, and he can stay at the servant's quarter backside of the bungalow." She knew that it was just an infatuation and the dog would also go somewhere in some time.

Pupu took the dog behind the bungalow, and with the help of the gardener, he bathed the dog - scrubbing him in the garden with the pipe kept for watering the plants. The dog was looking bright and beautiful now. Pupu was happy seeing him shaking fur to dry and shred the water. Pupu was jumping in happiness, and the dog was also dancing in response. Both soon became friends.

Pupu named him Tipsy.

Tipsy was well acquainted with kids behavior, and so he was behaving in a manner that his new master started loving him more. Fetching balls or sticks or flying discs were usual for Tipsy. He was smart in these games as he had always been busy doing the same with his previous master. Tipsy started following Pupu everywhere. But Tipsy knew that he was not allowed inside the house because he was told so by Pupu. Understanding such instructions were not tough for him because he had similar treatment earlier too. Some places in the previous master's house were also prohibited for him. But Tipsy was missing cozy comforts of the sofa and soft beds. He was made to stay under the gardener's cot on the ground. He disliked it. His fur and skin were itchy sometimes, and that disturbed him when he was sleeping.

One evening, when the car came in, Tipsy was looking from far. Pupu was out the whole day, and so Tipsy was waiting for him to meet and play. Pupu came out of the car running, and Tipsy also rushed towards him. Pupu hugged him and showed him a new neck belt and a bowl to eat in. Tipsy liked it very much and readily wore the new neck belt and got some food in the new bowl. Tipsy was happy to eat the food and was delighted that he no more had to eat roti, biscuits and other stuff thrown for him on the ground. Soon he was given a jute bag as his bed; he was content that at least he did not have to sleep on the floor anymore.

Tipsy and Pupu were good friends now. Pupu would care for Tipsy's food and well-being. With the nicest of the food and love and affection from the new master, Tipsy was gaining his health and glamour back. He had turned as beautiful and cute as he was in his previous master's house. Tipsy followed Pupu everywhere. Any guest that came to the house, Pupu ensured to introduce Tipsy as his best friend. Pupu's parents would also laugh but allowing Tipsy inside the house was still not okay with them. Pupu also never insisted in fear that his mom might ask Tipsy to be thrown out again. Pupu was happy that Tipsy was at least inside the compound, and both can spend time playing on the lawn in the garden.

One evening when Pupu was back from school, he could not even go and meet Tipsy as his parents were taking him to a fair. He was told that the fair was very big and there were lots of attractions for kids and adults both. They soon sat in the car and started to leave. Pupu saw Tipsy waiting for him at the far end of the garden. He shouted that he would be back soon to play with him. Tipsy rushed behind the car till the gate and stopped to see the car taking the first right. Tipsy waited for a while and looked around to see if he was being monitored. He again rushed towards in the direction of the car. He ran fast enough to catch the car, and he saw the car was waiting on the signal, but as soon as he reached, the car moved again as the signal turned green. Tipsy kept following till they reached the fair. But by the time he reached to the parking, he saw there was no one in the car. He wondered. Then he saw Pupu getting inside the fair from a huge gate. He rushed again to find himself lost in the crowd of the fair. He looked right and then left, he looked till the farthest end, but could not get a sign of his master. He started stumbling on one side and stopped at a place. He was deciding which direction to go. Suddenly, Tipsy found himself surrounded by some stray dogs. All of them started growling and grumbling on Tipsy.

Pupu was nearby and heard the dogs' noise and found Tipsy there. Giving no notice that his parents were moving ahead, he ran towards Tipsy to save him from the stray dogs. Tipsy was running and hiding under some pushcarts, but as soon as he saw Pupu, he ran towards him wagging his tail. This made the other dogs understand that he was with his master. But suddenly, Pupu realized that he was lost... He held Tipsy carefully and ran towards the lane he had just come from, but he saw no sign of his parents. He said to Tipsy that they were lost now and started crying.

On the other side, Pupu's parents also were searching for him. They ran all around, but could not find Pupu. They asked people and the shopkeepers but could not get a clue. At last, they reached the nearest Police patrol car to seek help. With two of the policemen, they searched again but failed to find Pupu. Policemen enquired the ticket collectors on the gate of the fair and some of the rickshaw pullers too. The policemen then asked Pupu's parents to go to the nearest police station so that they can send a message by wireless to all the police posts to be vigilant and notify about any lost boy.

Pupu's parents reached the police station and described the dress that Pupu was wearing, his age, complexion, hair and shoe color, etc. to help police identify him. They waited till 10 o'clock and then were asked by police that they will certainly try their best to find Pupu and bring him home, there was no point sitting in the police station. They were asked to go home.

Disheartened, they left for home. Pupu's mother was crying unstoppably. It was late in the night, and the roads were empty and dark. His mother's mind started questioning many things- "how will Pupu survive in this dreadful dark night? He must be hungry by now. What will he eat? Where will he eat? Where will he sleep? Has some gang picked him? What will they do with him?" She was continuously weeping.

As soon as they arrived home, the gatekeeper informed, "madam, Pupu has come home and ate his dinner and is sleeping now. He waited for you for long. You know the dog Tipsy has helped Pupu locate and reach home safely. Pupu was saying that Tipsy chased you to the fair."

He further added, "Dogs have a good memory and are good friends of human. Tipsy is a hero."

Both the parents were listening to this with their jaws open, and they got off the car hurriedly and rushed inside elated and saw

Pupu and Tipsy were sleeping together on the bed peacefully.

Activity: 3

Can you name some animals whom we can domesticate, make a pet? Do you know which animal was first domesticated by humane?

4
Worth of two rupees

Pupu was unhappy and not talking to anyone in the house. Pupu's financial worries were not taken seriously at home nowadays. And so he was on strike in his own way. He was staying in his office most of the day, and if anyone wanted to sneak a peek into his office, he shouted very loudly asking to leave him alone. He had stopped bringing in the newspaper for his father in the morning from the main gate of the house. He was not even looking out to know who was there on the gate for her mother during the daytime when someone rang the call bell. He was just seven years old, but he needed money to buy some articles for his office.

He had been behaving stubbornly recently. He would not listen to anyone's direction, neither would behave or be in discipline. He had lost mannerism too. His parents had been giving him whatever he wanted. This behavior of over-pampering had made Pupu stubborn. He kept demanding one or other things every day, and if not given he behaved very snappishly. His parents had started giving less importance to him and his demands these days to discipline him. They had stopped reacting over any of his tantrums too.

His office was one unused small tin box under a wooden table kept in the storeroom in the house. He sometimes covered the table from all around with a bed sheet and took his battery operated lamp to do his official work. The tin box was rectangular with a small lock to lock it. He possessed many articles in it. These were mostly the discarded things at home. Any shining piece of any broken crockery, cola bottle caps, empty matchbox, spring from the tic-tac pen, bobby pins, some old coins, and some colorful marbles. He ran his office between any hours of the day. He also kept one lord Hanuman postcard to keep him and his office safe from any miscreants. In his eyes, these miscreants were none but his guardians and parents at home because they thought his office and articles at his office were garbage and they wanted to get rid of them. His collection time was field duty for his office. His favorite spots were his grandfather's study room's dustbin. There he could find bookmarks, postage stamps on envelopes, some colorful visiting cards, rubber bands, colorful papers, etc. His family threw away stuff faster than he collected them. If they didn't do so, the heap of garbage would be as high as the nearest water tank. Whenever his articles were missing or thrown out, he would go on a hunger strike and talked to nobody at home. But soon he would be able to make his office up and running again. He certainly knew that nobody cared about his interests and all envied him and his office articles. Usually, after every wash out, he saw that the lord Hanuman postcard was never touched and remained in his box always.

He certainly knew now that be whatever may happen, the Lord Hanuman postcard was one thing no one would ever touch. He thought him to be a provider, a savior.

He wanted to visit the nearby temple to pray to Lord Hanuman. He wanted to pray for his office's safety and also to fulfill his financial requirement. Next day was Tuesday, and he planned to visit the Lord Hanuman in the temple. He got up early, took a bath, wore dhoti and took two *agarbatti*. His father was observing all these activities while sitting on the rocking chair with the newspaper in his hand.

Pupu reached the temple barefoot. He offered some flowers. Closed his eyes and with folded hands prayed – "O my dear lord Hanuman! Last time when I asked you for the red color compass box, you gave me a pencil box. I understand you might not be able to distinguish between them as you never had one in your childhood. But I accepted it. Before that, I asked you for a remote-controlled car, and you gave me a simple car. I understand there was no remote control when you were young. I again accepted it. So this time I am not asking you any article. I need money. I need money so that I can buy myself whatever I want. I won't confuse you anymore by asking for such things now. Do you think this is simple for you now? Please help me with some money. I can see you have received many cash today in *aarti*. I need only some, rest you can keep for your expenses. I understand, you also are bored of eating *laddoos* and fruits all the time and need to eat something else for the sake of a change of taste. Even I don't like eating the same *roti* and *subji* every day. I eat pizza and burgers sometimes. As a friend, I suggest you can also try. They taste good. Now I should take your leave. Please try fulfilling my prayer at the earliest. Thank you."

As soon as he entered his house, he saw his father was leaving for office. But he passed him without paying any heed to him. His father asked, "Where are you coming from, why are you barefoot? I am going to the office, will you not give me a hug today?"

He stopped for a while, and turned back, and hugged his father with no expression on his face, and no smile.

Upon which, his father caressed him and gave a pat on his back and kept something in his pocket and left for the office.

Immediately, Pupu ran into his office and tried to take out the money that his father kept in his pocket. He knew that it was a coin and it was a two rupees coin. He got disappointed and angry and thought, "Just two rupees, huh!"

He ran to the temple in anger and with his closed eyes and folded hands he said, "Hanuman Ji, I thought you are wise enough to read my mind. And so I did not mention how much money I need, this would look not very good, and you may think I am a greedy boy. Never ever you have given me sufficiently." With his big eyes and wide nose in anger he further said, "I am not keeping this two rupees and giving you back. I don't need this money." He kept the coin in a plate kept in front of Hanuman idol. And went home tramping his feet in anger.

He never received any money again, and then he dismissed the idea of getting money from anywhere. He got busy with other usual stuff in his everyday life. He knew he would not get money from anywhere.

Next morning, his uncle from Mumbai arrived. Pupu was very happy to see him because his uncle was a person whom he liked very much for the reason his uncle usually spent all the time with him. Pupu got answers for all his questions, be it as silly as why not animal wear clothes, or where does sun go in the night. His uncle also played games with him in his office. He received appreciation from his uncle for everything that he colored, and also for his sketches. He also got lots of chocolates.

When going back, his uncle gives him some money. This time he got a five rupees note. He was excited to know that finally his money need was heard. He thanked his uncle and saw him off.

He then directly ran to his office and opened his tin box. He looked around and kept thinking of the ways to spend his five rupees. He wanted a pencil with an eraser on its back. He wanted a pencil sharpener which was turtle shaped and collected the dirt within. He wanted a few stickers of some cartoon characters to stick to his tin box. He also wanted to buy one magnifying glass.

When his father had left for the office, he asked mom to take him to market to the stationary shop. He said he wanted to buy stuff.

His mother gave him a huffy look and said, "Why don't you go on your own, do you need your parents to help you buy things?"

She further added in a strong voice, "Kids who help their parent get help."

She further said she was not going to spend money on him, and she does not have any money.

On this unexpected reaction from her mother, he again shouted and said he was going to buy from his own pocket.

His mother gave him a roguish look and said she was not coming along if he kept talking in this manner. She further added that one should always be soft spoken and most importantly in the time of need. She questioned, "Why do you think I would come with you if you are speaking in such a rude voice?"

Pupu started weeping, feeling sorry for his actions, but he was still standing. *Sob... sob...*, "I want stuff, please mom, let's go to the shop."

Looking at his crying face and blubbering eyes, his mother got ready. Both of them reached to the shop.

He told the shopkeeper to give him the pencil, sharpener and selected some cartoon character stickers and also asked for one magnifying glass. He then extended the five rupees note to the shopkeeper.

The shopkeeper asked, "It is totaling to seven rupees, and so I need two more rupees."

Pupu had no money, and either had to leave some of the articles or give the remaining two rupees. He looked at his mom to grant him two rupees. But she rose her shoulder in refusal and ignorance.

With disappointment he turned and started rushing, his mother followed him. He was thinking something in his mind, and instead of reaching home he moved ahead towards the temple. His mother tried to stop him at home, but he did not stay. His mother also followed.

Soon he was standing in front of Hanuman idol and was howling and saying sorry to him. And soon his mother reached behind him and kept her hand on his shoulder. He then turned and narrated the whole story to his mother in his sobbing voice and said, "Now I know the worth of two rupees, and... and... *sob...sob...* also the value of smallest of anything that I have. I will stay happy with everything that I have and get, and will not be stubborn and demanding uselessly."

His mom gave him a tight hug and handed him a two rupees coin happily.

Activity: 4

Can you tell the currency notes and coins that are in circulation currently in our country?

5
Bahadur

It was past mid-night when Pupu opened his eyes to a sound of the thud of a stick on the road followed by a whistle and then followed by someone saying in heavy voice *jaagte raho* with stretch on both the words. Immediate he hid under his father's arm under the blanket and tightly closed his eyes.

He was trembling until the noise had completely faded and he was asleep again.

When he got up, he narrated his father what had happened the last night when everyone was fast asleep. He said, "Dad, you know there was someone on the road near our gate yesterday night, and he was making noises. He seemed to be a dangerous person, and so I did not wake you up. I too hid under the blanket. He also carried a thick stick it seems. And at times he was whistling and saying *jaagte raho* too."

Pupu's father while making him ready for school replied, "Oh! He is Bahadur. He is our night watchman. He keeps us safe from thieves at night. He stays awake whole night and stays watchful."

"Thieves? But how can he? He carries only a stick. How will he fight with thieves?" queried Pupu.

"How can he be fearless in the dark nights and go all alone? He must be ferocious by looks too, I think," he further added.

"That's why he is called Bahadur, meaning a brave man. He is not afraid of anyone in the night, unlike you do in darkness, and he is like us," his father replied.

"No, why will I fear the darkness, I don't" Pupu replied in buoyancy.

"Oh! Really? Let's test tonight. You will have to sleep in the verandah tonight. Can you do that?" his father asked.

Pupu replied immediately, "Sure Dad, but you know I got hurt yesterday as I fell off my bicycle, and I have hurt my knees. It is difficult for me to sleep on the hard surface."

"No problem, I will make your bed there tonight," his father sounded definitive.

"I have to sleep early tonight to get up and go to school; one can't sleep early in the verandah until everyone has slept and shops on the roads are closed. I should not wait until it is dark all around, it will be too late for sleep, and then I will be late in waking up too," Pupu replied to convince his father.

"Looks like you are afraid, but the verandah has an iron grill on all the side, and so it is safe. No one can enter," his father challenged him again.

"No, not at all, let me come back from school, and we can plan then," Pupu answered and quickly finished his breakfast and went to school. And thus he avoided facing any further question of challenges from his father.

When he came back from school, he stayed outside playing till late in the evening to avoid facing his father. His plan was to let his father go to the study room after coming from office and by the time he would arrive for dinner, Pupu would be sleeping under a blanket hiding from his father. And he followed the same suit.

"Get up, Pupu," his father called while stepping in the bedroom from his study room.

His father rolled Pupu in his bed and patted on his back to get up. He took Pupu's bed to the verandah and said, "Come with me."

Pupu got up and looked at his mom, hesitated for a moment, and followed his father. On the way, he threw a look of appeal at his mother. On this, his mother said, "That's fine now, let him sleep in the hall instead."

"Yes, let me sleep in the hall dad," Pupu pleaded.

"No. You must sleep on the verandah alone in the darkness. You must learn to be fearless. It is just a matter of one's habit, and one must have or get this during the course of time." You aren't a little kid anymore.

"I am ready to sleep alone but give a lamp please," Pupu again pleaded.

"No. You won't get a lamp; you have to sleep in the dark as everyone does. You also sleep in darkness when in the bedroom, there is no difference, you will know by morning," his father sounded strict.

"And remember, if you don't, I will make you laughing stock among your friends tomorrow," his father added further.

Pupu was pained, and he disliked the cruelty he saw in his father's nature. He sat on the bed made for him on the verandah and looked all around inside first and then outside to the big trees on the other side of the road. He felt he had been given a balustrade to stay in for no crime.

The trees were looking like giants in the night. No lights were coming through the trees like in the daytime, and so just shapes of trees were visible which appeared to him like dreading creatures. All the tree shapes to him were like the devils and ghosts from the stories he had heard from his mother or grandmother.

Initially, some people passed by the road, but soon there was complete silence. As the night advanced, he could listen to his own breath. He could hear many sounds coming from the far end of the earth. He tried sleeping but was unsure of his safety – 'should he keep his eyes closed to avoid looking all around and getting afraid? Should he keep his eyes open to be watchful and alert? Should he cover himself from head to toe under the blanket and keep his eyes open, or closed?' He was confused. After attempting all the ways, he decided to cover himself from head to toe and keep his eyes half open but uncovered. He wanted to stay awake, but soon he was asleep.

It was midnight when Bahadur started his duty. Bahadur's voice of *jaagte raho,* the whistling sound and the thud of the stick was approaching near; Pupu started shivering in fear. He thought it to be a dream, but gradually the sound was nearing him. Slowly he rolled his body in the corner and covered himself with the blanket. He opened his eyes slowly and glanced all around to feel safe, but Bahadur's voice was next to his ears now. Pupu peeped through his half-opened eyes and saw a hefty man wrapped in a shawl with a thick and long bamboo stick in one hand and a torch in another hand. He was flashing the torch to tear the darkest of all corners. And then suddenly, his torch flashed on to the verandah where Pupu was rolled in a corner.

"Who is hiding there? Just stay there," Bahadur challenged in a heavy voice and stood firm.

"It's me, it's me, Pupu... keeper of this house," Pupu replied as quickly as he can in shivering voice, uncovering his face.

By now Pupu has also seen Bahadur's face and recognized him. "You are the keeper of the park, aren't you? I have seen you in the park in the evening." Pupu said.

"Yes, I am the same. But what are you doing here at this time of the night? And why are you awake at this time?" Bahadur queried.

"Oh me, I was, I am, like you doing... sentinel of the house at night." Pupu lied and said in buoyancy.

Bahadur laughed "Ha! Ha! That's great; when I was young like you, I was afraid of darkness, you know."

"And you know, later I came to know that darkness is nothing but the absence of light, and everything remains the same. And from that day I have no fear of darkness," Bahadur added further.

"That's true, the absence of light is darkness. And so I am not afraid of darkness. That's why I told my father that I would be the guard of my house and preferred sleeping in the verandah so that if anyone dared to break in, I could challenge him," Pupu again exaggerated.

"I can sleep alone, in the night, in the verandah, you see. Also, I can go and fetch mangoes in the darkness from the orchard." Pupu seemed to be diminishing Bahadur's courage in front of him.

Bahadur was feeling interested in listening about Pupu. And Pupu was feeling comfortable with Bahadur in the darkness.

"You go and sleep now. I have to do my duty now. If you are sleeping here tomorrow, we can continue this conversation." Bahadur ended the conversation and started moving ahead.

"Okay, we'll surely meet tomorrow night again. It was nice talking to you," Pupu replied in confidence thinking how gratifying time he had just spent in the darkness and this could never have happened at daytime.

When Bahadur's voice had gone far, Pupu again started fearing. He thought, "Had Bahadur been here, I had not been afraid of darkness. Can I ask him to come here and stay here the whole night?"

He tried pulling the blanket to cover himself again, but he woke up to his surprise that the blanket had fallen off his body and completely from the bed. He seemed to be sleeping uncovered for the most part of the night. He looked around. He was in disbelief. He had opened his eyes to a new dawn, with birds chirping all around. He found nothing changed during the night. And that the dream has given him a new dawn, a beginning. A dawn, he saw spreading light and erasing darkness from all around and fear of darkness from within too.

Meanwhile, he saw his father coming from behind calling him to wake up "Bahadur ladke (brave boy), you have already got up!! That's fantastic..."and Pupu hugged his father and said, "Dad, it was great sleeping here and opening eyes to the beautiful dawn."

Activity: 5

Do a research about what is the brightest object in the sky immediately after the sunset and before the sunrise. It will be so interesting to know.

6

Booji

Pupu asked her mom, who was feeding milk to her younger son, "Mom, who is Booji? You keep telling my younger brother that Booji will come if he does not drink milk or eat food."

His mother laughed and said, "It's nobody, my child, I just want him to be afraid of something named Booji so that he drinks milk faster or eats properly. You know little ones get distracted easily and may not have proper food at times."

"No, no, you will have to tell me who is Booji, what does he look like? You are hiding something from me," Pupu insisted.

His mother went to the kitchen fondling him to serve dinner for herself and his father, telling him to sleep as his little brother was asleep now.

Pupu kept thinking about Booji.

Next day in his school, Pupu asked his friends about Booji, but none of his friends were aware. When he came home, he rang up his *Nani Ji* to ask about Booji, but he did not get a proper response. In the evening he went to play with friends in the playground behind the post-office, he asked his friends there too. Pupu also asked the keeper of the park and got a response that he did not know any boy or girl with this name. Wondering Pupu came home, and after dinner, he asked Google on her mom's smartphone. The google search result surprised him that it was a character created by one American band. It was a simian child and wore an orange nuclear protection suit. He thought Booji must be like a simian. He now knew that there was someone named Booji. But why did he come only when my younger brother was not eating or drinking milk, Pupu thought while he lay awake in his bed.

That night, he dreamt of a bizarre creature. He had hands and legs like a human being. But other features were not matching to a human.

The creature had no nose but only nostrils, mouth and eyes. His face was round in shape as if it was a pumpkin. And his body, especially the stomach was like a large football as if he ate a lot. His face was plain and had just two eyes balls with no eyebrows and eyelashes. He had no teeth but a long and thick tongue. When he was eating, it seemed that he did not have to chew but swallow only. And so he was quick in eating, also since his stomach was so big, he could eat a mountain like a heap of food. He saw this creature eating one meal equal to four meals. He saw him eating anything and everything edible coming on his way. Be it leaves, small plants, crops, fruits, vegetables, food waste on the streets, any cooked food, or anything -everything was his meal. He was unstoppable until he was getting the supply of food. He also ate ice creams, lollipops, biscuits, candies and sweets from children's hands or plates just by slurping with his long tongue. Children were afraid, and so were their mothers. Everyone was eating their food as soon as it was ready in their home.

Or they kept their food covered with a lid in a safe place to save it from Booji's eyes. Else, this creature would come in silently and would eat it all. The whole city was in terrible shock and fear. They had no clue how to get rid of this creature. They tried finding out who his parents were, but they could not. They tried finding where has he come from but they found rumors only that he was from the planet Mars. They also did not know where he went after eating food.

People reached to scholars and scientists, but they denied of any such creature ever found or mentioned in any literature. People could only find his name that too was a given name by people who have seen him.

They called him by the sound he made when he found any edible thing. He sounded *"aahha, ahaa BOOJI, aaha BOOJI"* whenever he found food, and he was delighted after eating. People were afraid to come near to him because of his stocky build. It seemed that he was very strong.

Pupu got up from his dream with a shock when he saw Booji was coming towards him to snatch and slurp his lollipop.

He did not tell his dream to anyone and went straight to the park after his breakfast. He was thinking that if at all a creature like Booji was real, then he had to save people around by making everyone aware of keeping their food safely covered and not throw waste in open that attracted Booji.

He saw that the keeper of the park was eating under a tree in the park. He went to him and narrated the whole story and said, "Booji can arrive at any time from anywhere." He also asked him to be aware and eat his food as soon as it was ready. If Booji saw it, he would eat it all.

The keeper of the park got stunned, and he ate his food quickly. And rushed to his house. He went straight to his kitchen covered all the food with lids. He called his wife and said, "look, now on we have to eat as soon as the food is cooked, and also be careful not to keep any food uncovered.

There is a beast in the town, no one knows where he comes from, and no one has the strength to stop him, he finishes the food when he sees it. He is a gourmand. He is called BOOJI." His wife was also dumbfounded after listening to her husband.

She immediately told the news to her neighbor. And it spread like a jungle fire. Booji was a known name in the neighborhood.

Soon, newspapers, radio, and television started covering the news. It became the talk of the town. Many people claimed that they had encountered Booji. They have seen him eating like a monster. Some claimed that he was 10 feet tall and was heavy like the Great

Khali, the WWE wrestler. Others said he is doughty and could jump as high as one storey building. Some said he was like a human, but others said he was like the hulk. Some said Booji came in the night; others said Booji attacked their kitchen in the daytime. There were as many stories as many mouths. It became a collective obsessional behavior. However, every story ended with the conclusion that food should be eaten immediately after it was ready and should always be covered to save it from Booji. And don't spread around anything, including waste, which can attract Booji.

It was the quarter end, and the local administration had been taking surveys every quarter in these localities. The administration had a new finding this time. They were shocked to see a drastic change in the behavior of the people living in these localities. The survey report was presented on the table of the district commissioner. The survey report was then tallied with the local dispensary and clinics. The shocking change that was found was in the newspaper the next day. Even the television and radio news followed to cover the story. The local administration and press named it the *"Booji Effect."*

Pupu's mom was reading aloud the newspaper for Pupu and his father with a smile the next morning. The newspaper read:

BOOJI EFFECT - These localities were mostly surrounded with a heap of dirt. Poor sanitation was a big reason for all the illness and related deaths. In the past, for many years, local administration kept on driving people to keep clean and cover their food and drinking water all the time. But nothing had changed since ages. Due to this, the colony had a bad record of diarrhea and related deaths of old aged men and children. And this time the survey has recorded a sharp decline in diarrhea and related mortality rate. BOOJI HAS ATE THE UNHEALTHY HABITS OF THE LOCALS.

Thank You BOOJI. We welcome you to visit the whole town.

Activity: 6

Do you know what can happen if we leave our food open, and if we eat it after several hours of cooking? Ask your mother to explain.

7
The wishing Banyan tree

This summer vacation, Pupu spent each day in the old Shiv temple with his Nani Ji. She was a daily visitor to the temple. The temple was behind the mines safety office building. The office building was on the opposite side of the main road, and Nani Ji needed help to cross the busy main road to reach the temple. So Pupu had assigned himself the job of escorting Nani Ji to cross the road to reach the old Shiv temple and bring her back. Nani Ji and Pupu both were very fond of each other.

Recently Nani Ji slipped from stairs and hurt her ankle. She visited a doctor and was given some medicine too, but the pain had only reduced, not gone forever. She had started limping a bit and walked slowly now. Due to this, she was not confident to cross the busy main road all alone to reach to the temple. She was blaming herself and her old age for not being able to visit the temple. Looking at this, Pupu extended help and both of them started going to temple. Nani Ji was happy with the support that Pupu has extended and blessed him always. Their bonding grew stronger. Nani Ji began to excusing Pupu for anything and everything and started saving him from his parents' rebuke too. Pupu too was enjoying his freedom in her patronage.

Going to the temple was an everyday activity. Earlier, Nani Ji was taking one hour to walk across the busy main road and offer worship in the temple and come back. The most time-consuming part was crossing the busy main road as it was always crowded by a variety of vehicles, trucks, bus, minibus, auto rickshaw, cycle, cycle rickshaw, and scooter.

The time to offer worship was just ten minutes. On the main road the traffic was fast, and sometimes people drove rashly too, which always frightened old aged people like Nani Ji.

Since Nani Ji had started going with Pupu, the time to cross the main road took only five to ten minutes; however their overall trip increased to over two hours. The main reason for this extended duration was Pupu's liking for the Old Banyan tree.

The Banyan tree was very old, and some quoted its age to the colonial era, but that was the age of the office building. It was a colonial building covered with thick maroon colored paint and designed with rectangular marks of bricks all over the outer wall. There was a wide verandah with pillars joining the arched designs. Others said that the age of the Banyan tree was older than the office building and much older than colonial age. The stem of the Banyan tree was as thick as five elephants standing together. The spread, though cut at times, was so large that it could cover two hundred people under it. The floor under the tree was cemented. And as very less sunlight tore the density of the tree on to the floor, there was always algae patches everywhere. The lowest branch of the Banyan tree could be reached by anyone after climbing the wall hedge surrounding the Banyan tree. The branch was long and so was springy. It was a nature-made swing. Pupu with other boys enjoyed the ride and always swung on that branch.

Pupu always got so engrossed in climbing the tree that he often ignored Nani Ji's call to go back home. And this always caused delay.

Pupu got so much fond of climbing the Banyan tree, riding the branch and swinging every day that he slowly lost interest in staying at home and doing his studies. He had been warned by his parents many times, but it never lasted long. If he was scolded and cautioned in the evening to refrain from stepping out of the house and going to the tree, the next evening, he would again be found hanging on the Banyan tree. It had been two months since his school had resumed after the summer vacation, but his fondness to the tree has not yet ended. Even if he had been to the temple with Nani Ji in the morning, he would again try going in the evening all alone. If he felt that his parents were watchful, he made some excuse to step out of the house and land to the Banyan tree at least for some time. Sometimes if he found the main gate locked, those times, he would jump across the backyard garden hedge and reach to the Banyan tree without anyone's knowledge.

One fine day when he was caught doing the same, he was beaten up by his mother severely. He kept weeping that evening. At last Nani Ji consoled him and fed him dinner and then took him to bed earlier than usual.

While on the bed Nani Ji told him about the Banyan tree. She said, "Do you know the Banyan tree that we worship is a wishing tree. You can wish anything from him, and that will be fulfilled. Next time when you go to the Banyan tree, make a wish for yourself."

"Like the wishing well in the story once you told? But what can I wish Nani Ji?" asked the curious boy.

"Exactly, like the wishing well. You can wish that you do well in your studies, you can ask to make you attentive in your studies," Nani Ji tried putting words of motivation towards his studies by her reply.

Next day Pupu almost missed the school bus because he came late from the Banyan tree from his usual morning trip to the tree. His mother was outraged and threatened to complain about his behavior to his father. He was afraid stepping out when he came from school. Nani Ji told him to stop going to the tree and stay home for his studies if he did not want to be scolded and beaten by his parents. She also reminded him that his examinations were going to start soon. She persuaded him by saying that the summer holidays time was over now and he should focus more on his studies. Pupu was upset and was looking for some excuse to step out and reach to the destination. And then it started raining which brought him more resentment that now he would not be able to step out. He had no option but to go and study. He sat on his study table near the bed. He kept his one eye on the book and other outside the window to keep a check on the rain. And to his fortune, the rain lasted soon. He peeped all around his house and saw everyone was busy with their work. He found this to be a good chance and tiptoed out for his adventure leaving his books and school bag open on his study table.

It was evening prayer time in the temple, and as soon as people came out of the temple after the prayer and *aarti,* they found Pupu fallen on the ground and was crying in pain. He was unable to stand up. He had fallen from the tree. The branch of the tree was wet and slippery due to rain. He was fearful of going home in this condition but had no option. Some acquaintances present in the temple helped him to reach his house. His mother was in shock after seeing him and questioned what had happened to him. She was surprised to realize that he managed to sneak out of the house, as per her, he was doing his studies all this while. People told that he had fallen from the Banyan tree. His mother was in tears looking at him and suddenly started scolding him, "you have been warned repetitively, but you never cared." She also added that this was the result of not being obedient. Pupu was looking at his mother with remorseful eyes. He was saying sorry to her and repetitively cry in pain. After a while, his father arrived from office and Pupu was taken to the doctor. His right ankle and thigh bones were fractured and needed a plaster from toe to thigh. After the plaster was done, he was advised not to move and give weight to the right leg for three weeks.

At home, he was rested on the bed near his study table. He was depressed more than the pain of broken bones. He kept quiet. He did not answer to any of his parent's questions in more than one or two words. Nani Ji was continuously cursing herself for his troubles. She sensed that the boy was depressed and so was trying to talk and make him feel relaxed. But he was not behaving normally. Three days passed but he hadn't got up for anything or asked anything except help in reaching the toilet. His mother was feeding him on the bed.

Fourth day morning, when Nani Ji came from the temple and gave him his favorite *prasad* mango to eat, he readily took it and told Nani Ji that he did wish for his studies and good marks but look what happened. He questioned, "Nani Ji, are you sure that the Banyan tree is a wishing tree? I hope you did not tell a lie to me. You know that evening I told my wish to the Banyan tree so that I can be focused on my studies but look what has happened, I broke my leg. I am not sure how I will do my studies now. I am not able to go to school. Don't you think the God in the Banyan tree has done wrong to me?"

"Oh ho, don't say all this, my child, God is great and does well for everyone. The Banyan tree fulfills your wish if you wished for it wholeheartedly," Nani Ji replied consoling him and caressing him on his head.

He ate the mango and enjoyed it. The joy of eating mango gave him a break from his boring bed-rest time. Mango could even bring life to dead. He got up a little by putting pillows under his waist. He looked around. He could see outside the window and the door. It was the rainy season now, and he felt good as he saw the backyard lawn and trees through his window. They were all clean and washed and so green. He turned to the other side and saw his school bag on his study table just within his reach. He pulled the school bag on the bed and took out all the books. All of them were new. The session for his standard three has just started. He could feel the pleasant aroma of the new books. He had not been able to see all the books and all the pages of the books since he had been busy hanging on the Banyan tree. He picked his English reading book and turned the pages. The title of the stories and pictures on the pages attracted him. He started reading stories. He liked the first story. He read the second story. And then saw some questions after the second story. He turned the page to the first story and found questions at the end of that story too. He then started answering the questions, and then also answered questions in the second story. He found it exciting work. His oxytocin supply was to the fullest. He turned other books and their pages too during the day and was feeling very content after completing chapter from any of the book. He felt a great accomplishment in doing so.

His father and mother also noticed his changing interest. Nani Ji was bringing *prasad* for him every day and caressed him for being so devoted. His father started spending time everyday evening to solve Pupu's queries and also to help understand any complex mathematics problem and science theory. Pupu was happy with the attention that was given to him. He started feeling a sense of responsibility to return the best that he could to his parents.

By the time he reached the third week, he had no guilt feeling that he won't be able to do his studies and may flunk in his examination. He was taken to the doctor; an x-ray was taken and found to be good. He was relieved from the hospital immediately after his plaster was cut. He was looking forward to starting his school from the next day.

He started going to school. After some days he got his result of the unit tests held. He was appreciated by the class teacher for his good marks despite suffering a loss of class. While coming back from school, he felt blissful and couldn't wait to announce his result to his parents and Nani Ji. He looked outside from the window of the bus nearing his house, the treetop of the Banyan tree was visible. He kept his eyes on the treetop while the bus was moving ahead and slowly closed his eyes. With his closed eyes he was wishing not to get broken bones again while climbing the Banyan tree.

Activity: 7

Banyan Tree is the National tree of India and state tree of Madhya Pradesh. The Thimmamma Marrimanu Banyan tree in Anantapur in Andhra Pradesh has Guinness record of being the largest tree specimen. Can you find biggest and oldest Banyan trees of India?

8

The thief monkey in the zoo

Pupu asked his father "How many animals are there in the jungle?"

His father replied, "There are many. I will take you to the zoo. You can see many birds and wild animals there."

Next Sunday, his father took him to the zoo.

First, Pupu saw a monkey jumping and making noises and faces at the visitors. Next, he saw an alligator taking a sunbath. When he moved ahead, he saw an elephant. The elephant was very happy because he was taking a bath, he was filling his trunk with water and splashing it on himself like a shower. Meanwhile, one monkey came to take the elephant's banana. He was hungry. But the elephant was watchful and splashed the water from his trunk on the monkey to make him beware that he was being watched. Wet and afraid, the monkey could not take the bananas. It was amusing to see the act between the elephant and the monkey. Monkey seemed to be a mischievous thief. All the zoo visitors including the parents of the kids laughed to see the mischievous monkey thief. It looked like he had come out of his cage somehow. He was trying hard to take away other animals food too.

Pupu moved ahead to see a lion. Pupu was too scared to see the lion. The lion was resting on the top of his cave. Some boys tried waking him up by making funny noises. The lion looked around and roared. Everyone got scared by his roar. Pupu thought that the lion would jump and cross the cage to eat every visitors because they have disturbed the king of the jungle. But then his father said that the cage was built such that the lion can't jump and cross the distance. His father said that they were safe until they fell into the cage. Father's words were unbelievable because the lion was so mighty that he could jump big and high, but since he knew his father always told facts, Pupu believed.

Next, Pupu saw a lake filled with many goose, cranes and other birds living near the lake. They had very long legs and long beaks too. Their wings were also significant. All of them were making the quack-quack sound. He also saw a few brown ducks swimming in the lake. These were good swimmers. They were taking a dip at one point and after some time coming out from a far distance. They were covering a long distance while swimming under the water.

There was one reptile park too. They saw some cobra snakes and chameleon, and a very fat and big python. Some pieces of meat were kept near him. All of the reptiles were sleeping. His father told him that it was their time of hibernation, a phenomenon when snakes and some other reptiles slept and stayed inactive in cold weather. Only one of the snakes, which was thin and green in color, was moving to reach to the top of the tree within the cage.

When they came out of the reptile park, they heard some noise. They rushed towards the noise and saw that the zookeepers were behind the monkey which had come out his cage and trying to steal others food. Zookeepers were trying to bring the monkey down from a tree by showing him some guavas and bananas. But the monkey was very smart. When zookeepers were keeping the fruits near the tree to trap the monkey, the monkey came down, but as soon as he saw the zookeepers approaching, he climbed back to the top of the tree. Some zookeepers hid behind the bush to trap the monkey, but this game of hide-and-seek went on for more than an hour. People wanted to know why were they behind this monkey, why couldn't they let him go. The zookeepers said that this monkey had been stealing the fruits from the store and also from the animals. "Every day we were surprised to see the depleting fruits from the stores. We certainly knew that it is an act of a monkey as we found peels of bananas and other fruits that he was eating in the storeroom. So it is very important to catch this monkey and put back in the cage."

After many failed ways and attempts to catch the monkey, it was decided to tranquilize him. Soon the monkey was tranquilized and left in the cage with other monkeys. Other monkeys were not nearing him as he was unconscious and were only giving a surprised look from far, unlike their behavior. Usually, monkeys gathered around to pay respect to a dead monkey, they hugged each other and console. But this was not happening. The keeper of the zoo was watching them with suspecting eyes. After a while, the monkey woke up and then the other monkeys started making noise and some trying to kick him too. Soon the monkey was cornered. Next day when the zookeeper came to feed them, he saw the monkey was sitting far away from the group. Soon they realized that the monkey that they had caught was actually not from the zoo. He might have come from outside seeing the greenery and trees. Also, he seemed to be a trained monkey and might be with some madari from where he had escaped. The zookeeper went close to the monkey and tried communicating something in sign language and some verbal words too. To this, the monkey gave a proper response and tried communicating back. The message was clear to the zookeeper that he was not from the zoo and wanted to be freed from the cage. The zookeeper immediately opened the cage and took out the monkey and tide him to a rope, unlike other monkeys he was not trying to get free from the rope. The monkey was then kept out of the cage but tied to a long rope at a faraway tree. The monkey was daily given a bunch of bananas to eat. The monkey was happy swinging on the tree branch and visitors were happy seeing a monkey swinging and jumping branch to branch, tree to tree eating bananas like the Tarzan.

Activity: 8

Do you know Apes are not monkeys? Can you find out what is the difference between apes and monkeys?

Sneak peak into next book by Amitabh Sinha

Pupu is very courageous and dares to investigate things around him. He now looks up everything and everywhere to know what is unknown to him, to get all the aspects of anything that he confronts. He is now very sure that everything has some or other phenomenon attached to science. He has understood the existence and importance of science in life. He knows one can explain things with the help of logic, and that logic is science.

Let's know more of his journey in the next series where he explores scientific experiments and facts in "Getting along with Friends, family, and neighbor with Pupu."